THE SLOW NORRIS

Making Friends

Hippo

Scholastic Children's Books,
Commonwealth House, 1 – 19 New Oxford Street, London WC1A 1NU
A division of Scholastic Limited
London – New York – Toronto – Sydney – Auckland

Published by Scholastic Limited 1996
Copyright © HTV Ltd 1995
Illustrations copyright © Arkadia 1996
Based on The Slow Norris television series created by Dan Maddicott

Text adapted by Gabby Goldsack

ISBN 0 590 19042 3

Printed by Printek in Spain

10 9 8 7 6 5 4 3 2 1

It was a warm, sunny day. Allie found herself wandering through a strange wood. It was very odd. She didn't know where she was, but she had the strangest feeling she knew exactly where she was going.

Soon she came to a signpost. "Follow ... your ... nose!" it said.

And a little further on there was another signpost, at the foot
of a hill. It read 'Best foot forward'.

"That's all very well," said Allie, "but both my feet are as good
as each other. So I shall just have to skip."

Allie skipped up the hill. But suddenly she stopped. There was a strange grunting sound coming from somewhere. "Hmmm ... it sounds like there's something *inside* this hill," she thought. "But how could it get inside?"

By now she had reached the steep side of the hill, and was amazed to find something that looked like a door knocker. Cautiously she picked it up.

KNOCK! KNOCK! KNOCK!

Inside the hill the knocks echoed around a damp and dismal cave. The knock woke up the huge hairy creature in the cave. He was puzzled.

KNOCK! KNOCK! KNOCK!

There it was again. The creature lumbered towards the sound.
Trembling, it pressed its ear against the door.

"Is there anybody there?" called Allie. "Hello ... hello? Does this open? Is this a door?"

"What's a door?" asked the creature in a low, slow, lugubrious voice.

"It's the thing you open to let me in," replied Allie.

"Who's **me**?" asked the creature.

"I am!" said Allie

"Oh then who am I?" asked the creature, scratching his head.

By now Allie, who was very curious and getting a little impatient, had begun to push at the door. Suddenly it gave way and the creature was catapulted across the cave.

"Aaargh. Who are you?" they both shrieked when they came face to face.

"I'm Allie," said Allie.

"What's an Allie?" the creature frowned.

"I am, silly," said Allie.

"You're silly? But I thought you said you were Allie.

"Oh dear, let's start again," laughed Allie. "My *name* is Allie."

"What's a name?" asked the creature, who was becoming more confused by the minute

"A name is ... well, it's what you call a thing or a person," replied Allie. "Now let me see," she said, casting her eyes around the cave. "This is called a table ..." she said, patting the table.

"A table," repeated the creature.

"And this is a saucepan," added Allie, who was beginning to enjoy herself. "Stop me if I'm going too fast."

"Stop," said the creature. "You're going too fast."

Allie went on naming this and that in the cave until suddenly she did stop. She had noticed the word 'Norris' written on the end of the bed.

"And you must be ... The Slow Norris," she said triumphantly.

"Why must I?" asked the creature.

"Because you're very slow and it says Norris on your bed," replied Allie.

The Slow Norris stood still and listened. "Well, I can't hear it," he said.

"That's because the word is written down. Look ... 'Norris'!" she explained, pointing at the writing. "Words are things that you can say or write. Words are made up of letters. Do you know your ABC?"

"No. What's my ABC?" asked The Slow Norris, shaking his head slowly.

"It's a ... well, you know!" said Allie.

"No, I don't," replied The Slow Norris.

"You really should get out more," laughed Allie.

"There's an 'out'?" The Slow Norris asked in surprise.

"Of course there's an out! I came in through it, remember?" exclaimed Allie, who was getting a bit exasperated by the silly creature.

"You're the only one who ever did," said The Slow Norris.

"Well, how do your friends get in?" asked Allie.

Norris scratched his head and looked thoughtful. "What's a friend?" he asked.

For the first time since meeting The Slow Norris, Allie looked as if she really could not believe her ears. "You must know what a friend is," she spluttered.

"Must I?" replied The Slow Norris.

"Yes," said Allie.

"Is a friend a little, round juicy thing that The Slow Doris likes to eat?"

"No," sighed Allie. "And it's Slow *Norris*, not Doris!" she added, shaking her head in amazement.

"Oh well. Then it must be one of those thorny sticks The Slow Boris scratches his fleas with," he said helpfully.

"It's not Boris ... it's Norris!" chuckled Allie.

By now poor old Slow Norris was getting quite desperate. "Is this a friend?" he cried, grabbing a spoon. "Oh well, what about this?" he asked, picking up a spider for Allie to see.

Allie shook her head and smiled kindly. "You really are very slow aren't you?" she said gently.

"No," said The Slow Norris. "Err ... What was the question?"

It was all becoming too much for him so he curled up into a tight ball and peered at Allie through his fingers.

"The question was," said Allie patiently, "what is a friend?"

"Well, I don't know! That's why I asked you," said The Slow Norris, who was beginning to feel quite sorry for himself.

"Ohhh! You are impossible," said Allie, who was beginning to think that Slow Norris was the silliest thing she had ever met.

"Er, this friend ..." began The Slow Norris.

"Yes?" said Allie impatiently.

"Would I like it?"

"A friend isn't an it. It's a somebody," explained Allie.

"Not just anybody?" asked The Slow Norris.

"Anybody can be a friend," said Allie. "But a friend is some-body special."

"I haven't got a somebody. I haven't even got an anybody. All I've got is a nobody," said The Slow Norris plaintively.

Allie looked up at The Slow Norris and took one of his large paws in her hand. "Do you want to make friends?" she whispered kindly.

"Um ... yes I do. Only what shall I make them with? I have got some wood and glue ..." The Slow Norris was obviously still very confused.

"You've got it wrong again," sighed Allie. "You can't make friends out of wood and glue. You make friends by being kind and making somebody happy ... Now look here," she said taking a small book out of her satchel.

"Where?" said The Slow Norris.

"Here in my magic book," explained Allie. "If you look hard enough, you can see anything you want to see."

"Oh," gasped Norris as he peered deep into the book which rippled and glowed with beautiful colours.

This is the story of how Jane the Fairy teaches Ferdy the Frog all about friendship.

"I'm such a goody two-shoes, always sensibly dressed!" exclaimed Jane the Fairy to Ferdy the Frog. "And I don't know any rude words!

Ferdy does know some rude words, and whispers them to Jane. She is shocked!

Jane the Fairy points out a lovely red butterfly with a broken wing. All Ferdy can think of is butterfly on toast or butterfly burgers!

Ferdy realises that the butterfly is actually Madame Butterfly – an old friend who once saved his life.

Ferdy remembered that he was washed up on a dry stone. Madame Butterfly had flapped her wings to keep him cool until the rain came.

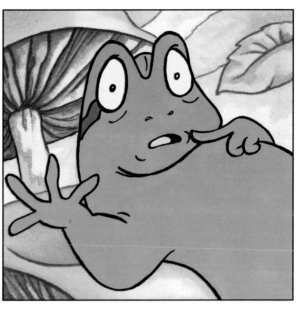

"Don't die, Madame Butterfly, don't die!" says Ferdy the Frog.

"We have to look after her. We can be her wings and take her home to safety."

That's what friends are for!

When the story ended, The Slow Norris sat in a thoughtful daze. Then he wandered over to his bed and searched around. Eventually he found what he was looking for. A huge, dirty, holey old blanket.

"This. This is my friend," he said, dreamily wrapping himself in the blanket.

"A smelly, rotten old blanket?" spluttered Allie in disgust.

"Smelleee? Rotten?" cried Norris. "No! No! Warm! Soft! Cuddly! Safe!"

Allie looked on in amazement as Norris rolled awkwardly around the floor in his blanket. Suddenly she burst into giggles and cried, "You are the silliest creature. You might be a Slow Norris, but you make friends very quickly."

The Slow Norris stopped rolling. "Do I?" he asked in surprise.

"Yes!" replied Allie, still laughing.

"Oh ..." said The Slow Norris, and slowly stood up.

"What's wrong?" said Allie.

"Well, where are they?" asked The Slow Norris.

"Where are who?" asked Allie, very puzzled.

"My friends," said The Slow Norris.

"Well, they're here, silly," chortled Allie.

"Where?" demanded The Slow Norris, squinting around.

"Me, silly. I'm your friend," cried Allie.

The Slow Norris shook his head and blinked in wonder. "You ... are my friend? You are the friend of The Slow Norris? But I haven't done anything for you. I haven't even offered you so much as a slug to eat."

Then The Slow Norris sat down and put his head in his hands. He looked like he was going to cry.

"Oh Slow Norris," cried Allie. "You don't have to do anything for me to be my friend. I know you're my friend because you cheer me up. You make me laugh."

"Laugh?" repeated The Slow Norris.

"Yes! You know ... ha! ha! ha!" said Allie

The Slow Norris scratched his head then said, "Ha? Ha? Ha? Oh! Yes, yes, I see!"

As they both started laughing, Allie took The Slow Norris's huge paw in her hand and they danced around the cave. The Slow Norris laughed so much that his eyes began to water! He'd never been so happy in his life!